Charles Hayden Proctor

The Life of James Williams, Better Known as Professor Jim

For Half a Century Janitor of Trinity College

Charles Hayden Proctor

The Life of James Williams, Better Known as Professor Jim
For Half a Century Janitor of Trinity College

ISBN/EAN: 9783337054304

Printed in Europe, USA, Canada, Australia, Japan

Cover: Foto ©Raphael Reischuk / pixelio.de

More available books at **www.hansebooks.com**

THE

LIFE OF JAMES WILLIAMS,

BETTER KNOWN AS

FOR HALF A CENTURY

JANITOR OF TRINITY COLLEGE.

BY

C. H. PROCTOR,

A MEMBER OF THE CLASS OF '73.

HARTFORD:
CASE, LOCKWOOD & BRAINARD, PRINTERS.
1873.

DEDICATED

TO THE INTERESTS OF THE

Worthy Servitor

WHOSE NAME APPEARS ON THE

TITLE PAGE.

I.

"I say the tale as t'was said to me."—SCOTT.

1*

LIFE OF

"PROF. JIM."

⁂

In tracing out the life of the venerable janitor whose name is so familiar to the alumni of Trinity College, we are taken backwards in time to a period of which few men now living have any remembrance; chiefly because "Prof. Jim" has advanced beyond the years allotted to man's portion, and his younger days were passed amidst scenes which have become historic.

He does not celebrate his birthday, mainly because he hasn't the faintest idea of the time of its recurrence, or even of his age at all, but certain data remain fixed in his mind, and a simple calculation will give his approximate age. He says, "I distinctly remember wearing a smock-frock and belt, and playing about the door-yard of my master's house, when I heard bells a ringin' and cannons a firin', and I ran in and asked my mother what was the matter, and she said, 'Why, Washington's dead.'" Other circumstances connected with his life a few years later, indicate that Jim was born about the year 1790.

He was the third of six children, and his mother was a French Creole, a slave belonging to a retired Revolutionary officer, one Col. Robert, who owned a large estate in Yonkers, New York. His father was a freedman, and did not even live in the same town with Jim's mother, but in Nyack, and although he visited his wife frequently, coming up the river in his own boat, yet he would return again shortly to his own home; he did not live with his family until Col. Robert gave his wife her freedom. A number of years of Jim's early life were passed in Yonkers and New York city, but as he expressively terms it, all those places have "*outgrowed*" him, and *his* New York is not the city of this generation.

New York city, according to an enthusiastic writer of the beginning of the present century, was then a beautiful town about four miles in length, situated at the foot of Manhattan island.

The principal streets were *Pearl street*, *Broadway*, and *Greenwich street*. "These run the whole length of the city, and are intersected, though not at right angles, by streets running from river to river. Pearl street, near the East river, pursues a narrow and devious course through a populous part of the city, and is the seat of great business. Broadway passes in a straight line over the highest ground between the two rivers, and is the noblest avenue of the kind in America. Greenwich street pursues a nearly straight course between Broadway and the Hudson, and is wide and elegant. *Chatham street* is a noble spaceway leading from Broadway into Bowery road. *Washington street* is a splendid avenue near the Hudson.

"The streets are generally well paved, with good sidewalks, and every part of the city is well supplied with lamps.

"The *Park* is a beautiful promenade of about four acres, on the south side of Broadway, and near the center of the city.

"The modern houses in New York are mostly of brick, and are generally well built; many of them are elegant. Among the public edifices are now included more than one hundred churches, which are occupied by the various denominations for religious worship. The steeple of St. Paul's is probably not excelled by any in the Union. The front of the new church in Wall street is handsome. The City Hall, situated at the head of the Park, is a noble specimen of architecture, and one of the most superb buildings in the United States.

"The number of houses in the city of New York in 1800 amounted to about 20,000, and the population to 100,000."

Yonkers was a series of plantations, and the beautiful town with which most of us are familiar, was hardly dreamed of in those days.

Col. Robert was a hard-working man, and although one of the wealthiest in that part of the state, and the largest slaveholder in the neighborhood, owning nine working hands, yet he worked with his men, and was very strict, enforcing constant labor "from sun to sun." He did not depend wholly on his own household for assistance in the fields, but employed about twenty men besides during the haying and harvesting season.

Prof. Jim testifies to the kindness of his master in providing food and clothes for his slaves, and in supplying comforts to them from his own table: and after making due allowance for the propensity of slaves to magnify their master's social position, we can conclude that Col. Robert was a man of some distinction. That he was intimately connected with men prominent in the politics of the day Jim firmly insists, and declares that he has himself, at his master's direction, driven from New York to Croton many a time, posting bills and circulating pamphlets advertising the candidates for election in whom his master was interested. Aaron Burr was one of these intimate friends of Col. Robert, and it was at the time he was nominated as candidate for the Presidency in 1800, that Jim was most busy. He says, "I'd ride night and day and all over the country east and west. I've been out carrying papers in a storm from midnight until one o'clock the next day, to Westchester and White Plains, and then with change of horses to Croton. I remember coming one day from Sing Sing at midnight, and being sent off again to the city, and I'd as lief go anywhere else as there, for the *Commons* was where the great Park is now, and about five miles out of town there were plenty of robbers and wild cattle." He remembers the rejoicings and celebrations of this year at the time of Jefferson's election, and declares that such a "barbecue" was never seen before at Yonkers as took place then, when an ox weighing fourteen hundred pounds was roasted whole. The snow was very deep, extraordinarily so for the season of the year, and the thousands of people assembled there were obliged to wade and stumble about in drifts waist high, and altogether there were so many things connected with this celebration that were strange and out of the way, that Professor Jim thinks that it would be impossible for one having seen it to forget it.

In the boyish days of our hero, the mischief which even now occasionally manifests itself, had, we may be sure, full sway, and he relates several incidents in which he was a moving spirit, with so much relish and so many hearty laughs, that one cannot resist joining him in his merriment.

He declares that his suspicions were often aroused at the sight of a big black bottle which stood in the closet of his missus' room, and says, "I made up my mind I'se goin' to see what was in that ar. Ole missus was asleep, and I was smellin' of the bottle and found it was gin, and so 'gan to want a taste, and had no sooner got the bottle to my mouf and smack-smack, when, 'Boy, what are you doin' there?' and she jes' took me out to the kitchen, and my mother gave me worse than three or four drinks of gin. Oh! I tell you that thar was music—that thar was music."

His mother obtained her freedom somewhat in this way; if Jim's statement is true, the relations of master and slave, to say the least, were very peculiar.

Col. Robert in a moment of anger struck one of the slave children, and Jim's mother immediately rebelled and flew to its protection; the master's son upheld the mother, and the master himself at length yielded; but the mother was not satisfied, and at length begged Col. Robert to send her away to some other slaveholder, and finally obtained the requisite pass, as she supposed it was, to leave her old home to go to some neighboring land-holder; but she discovered to her astonishment that the paper in question gave her her freedom.

Prof. Jim says that he himself was always a favorite, and to his recollection he was never whipped by his master but once, and then "after two licks with a dry alder, the stick broke, and that was enough."

"But did your mother never whip you?" "Oh, jolly! if my mother once got hold of me, then I tell you I saw stars."

Aaron Burr was a frequent visitor at Col. Robert's house, and a room was always ready for him, as he might stop at any time on his way from Albany to New York, or back again. The establishment of Burr seems to have made a strong impression on Prof. Jim's mind, and he describes with admiring tones the enormous carriage drawn by six horses, and the retinue of outriders and footmen which always accompanied him. Burr himself, Jim describes as a short, rough, and ugly man, who swore and cursed constantly, but who in ladies' society was very polite and exquisite.

(By the way of parenthesis we would like to add that a prominent gentleman in New York sees fit to deny Jim's assertion respecting the profanity of Aaron Burr. He says that after a long personal acquaintance with Burr, he was led to suspect nothing of the kind, and in his opinion this story should be taken *cum grano salis*.

In reply, we would say, we do not like to contradict Professor Jim's statement, when we find such authorities as Parton and Davis declaring plainly that the reason for the break between Washington and Burr, and the loss to Burr of his position in the army, was simply owing to his inordinate use of foul and profane language.)

At the time of the duel between Burr and Hamilton, Jim was at work in the fields at mail time, and his mother was sent on horse-back for the batch of papers which was due. She gave the letters, on her return, to her master, and he had scarcely read the first one he had opened, when, all hurry and excitement, he shouted, "Get a room ready quick, for that little devil is coming." When afterwards he learned that Hamilton had been killed in the duel, the excitement increased.

A moment's digression here to the statements of history will be serviceable in ascertaining how far Prof. Jim remembers this event. None of the several historians whose works were at our disposal, mention Burr's whereabouts immediately after the duel. All agree that he stayed somewhere near the city of New York, and it is conjectured that he remained at his family residence, Richmond Hill. "On Wednesday morning, the 11th of July, 1804, Burr and Hamilton met on the heights of Weehawken, and the duel was fought. On Thursday, the 12th, General Hamilton died, and on Saturday, the 14th, he was interred with military honors."

Burr writes to Joseph Allston, Esq., from New York, July 13th: "Gen. Hamilton died yesterday. I propose leaving town for a few days, and meditate also a journey for some weeks, but whither is not resolved. Perhaps to Slatesburgh. You will hear from me in about eight days."

The next letter with any date is from Philadelphia, July 29th.

Parton, in his life of Aaron Burr, says that immediately after the duel, Burr went to his home in New York (Richmond Hill), and for eleven days stayed at or *near* this place, writing, under cover of friends in Philadelphia, to his daughter and to his son-in-law. Jim's statement, as will be seen, becomes an important one in the history of Burr's life, inasmuch as the missing link in the broken chain of circumstances connected with his history from just before the duel till some weeks after, is here supplied. The interest attached to the account of the events in the life of our aged janitor increases, when we find ourselves able to verify his statements by means of the accepted statements of historians. We find as we proceed in this biography, that more than once we are able to refer to standard works for a verification of statements which, taken by themselves, might seem to the incredulous creations of Prof. Jim's fancy.

Now Jim says, " Burr went first to his own house in New York, Burr's Woods they called the place, near the old State's prison on West Broadway. The next day, between three and four in the afternoon, as we were putting up a new yard fence, there appeared a great cloud of dust away down the road ;

some one said that it was somebody riding, for the day was so quiet it could not be the wind. By-and-by a man came up and gave a note to master; that said he was coming. Pretty soon he came up himself in his four-horse coach, and drove into the yard and came out of the coach. His head was bowed down, and he didn't say a word; but then his head was always bowed down. He caught right hold of my master's hand, and they went into the house, and we didn't see him again till the next evening. The day that Hamilton was buried was a bad day for him, and he didn't eat any dinner, nor go out for his walk along the river, but he walked to and fro along the corridor up stairs, with his hands behind him. We could hear the funeral guns sounding up from New York.

"Burr kept his servant in the room with him night and day, and he had a case of pistols and a sword in his room with him. He stayed with my master some time, and practised a good deal at target shooting down by the river bank, and I myself have seen a white birch tree where there were twelve balls in a space as large as my hand. He left Yonkers for New York in a row-boat piloted by an Indian.

"I saw him several times after this in the city, when I went there to live, and he would often recognize me."

It seems that one time while Burr was at Yonkers he narrowly escaped being seized, for he was with

Col. Robert on one side of a garden hedge while two horsemen stopped on the other side in the main road, and remarked that "Burr was in Albany, and they were after him," and but for the expostulations of Robert, Burr would have shot at these men, and thus have declared his hiding place.

This is Jim's story of his connection with Burr, and throws aside entirely the number of little romances that students have delighted in; but as we have Jim's own word for the statement as given, we are *per force* obliged to give up the "carriage story" and that of his own presence on the field at the meeting of the duellists.

II.

"The sundry contemplation of my travels."

—AS YOU LIKE IT.

* *

Soon after the duel between Burr and Hamilton, Col. Robert died, and about a year afterwards, with the settlement of the estate, Jim went to live with a daughter of the Colonel, to whom he had been given by will. She lived in New York city, at No. 10 Dey street. His sister was a maid and he a servant for several years in the family of Miss Robert. They did not remain in the city the entire year, but during the summer months the family was broken up, part of them going to the "Springs" in a sort of caravan, for it was unsafe in those days to travel except in large companies, and stage coaches and private "establishments" were the only means of getting about the country, and the remainder spending the season in Yonkers.

The first summer, while the family were at the Springs, Jim was put out to work on a farm, and on the return of the family in the fall he went back again to his place as servant at Miss Robert's house. The various stories he heard from his sister, who of course traveled with her mistress, and the accounts he often received from a sister of his late master, of the beauties of the places which they had visited during their summer trip, incited Jim very much to go off by himself and prove the reality of these wonderful stories.

The thought worked upon his mind so much that before the next summer had arrived he was fully decided to see the world. When the family had determined to leave the city they placed Jim in the wholesale grocery store of Robert B. Lloyd, Esq., on Broadway; but Jim had his mind prepared for travel, and he seized the first opportunity, and with his bundle under his arm, ran away, managing to possess himself of sufficient money to pay his steamboat passage to New London, Conn. He says this steamboat was the *Fulton*.

He managed to get employment as hostler, for he had had some experience with horses while he lived in New York; but he was not satisfied, this wasn't the part of the world he was very much interested in, or at least he hadn't a realizing sense of its beauties, and the first instant he could get away, he shipped on board a West India trader, with a Capt. Fox.

On his return from this voyage he landed in New York, and went immediately on board an American ship, the *Eliza Gracie*, bound for Liverpool. From this voyage dates the adventurous part of Jim's life. On the day that they were about to land, having crossed the ocean, a rough, suspicious-looking schooner came along side the Gracie, and with scarcely any warning, boarded her with half a dozen men, armed with broadswords. They seized Jim, with three other men, and pressed them into service, carrying them off to the British sloop of war, the *Shepherdess*, which lay at anchor in the channel. "For over three years," says Jim, "I didn't put my foot ashore; I always had a hard time, and once I hit an officer."

The *Shepherdess* cruised about the American coast, generally in the Southern waters, and then again re-crossed the ocean and cruised about the shores of Africa in the Mediterranean, and again in the South Atlantic. At one time they sailed for six days up the Congo river, and the weather was so extremely hot that the crew suffered intensely. It became necessary to soak their shirts in oil several times a day, and even to rub their bodies with oil, to keep their flesh from burning.

The Captain of the *Shepherdess* had undertaken this voyage up the Congo from mere curiosity, and he almost lost his vessel by the rapidly running tides, which, in one instance, nearly carried them over the falls, where it would have been certain destruction. While at anchor at the mouth of the Congo river, Jim went on shore, wearing over his shirt a navy coat ornamented with large brass buttons. The naked inhabitants of that region no doubt thought the blue-coated sailor was some sort of strange animal, akin to their own species, yet altogether too highly ornamented to please their cultivated tastes, and before he was well aware of his situation, Jim found himself surrounded with dancing savages, howling what might have been his death knell for all he knew. He ascertained very shortly, however, that it was not so much his valuable person that they coveted, but only the bright buttons on his coat, and he readily sacrificed the article and escaped with his life, thankful for small favors.

What they ever did with those brass buttons is beyond Jim's conjecture.

While in the Mediterranean, they once landed on the shores of Turkey, and at another time witnessed a battle, which Jim insists was between a party of Greeks and some of their enemies. Jim asserts that the Captain would not allow much flogging, and in his case punishments of this sort came very seldom, for, says the Captain, "Let him alone, he is one of the Yankee cow-boys." During the war of 1812, the *Shepherdess* came back to the United States, and made a trip up the St. Lawrence river to Quebec, then back along the coast to New York.

At the time of the fight between the *Chesapeake* and the *Macedonian* and *Guerrière*, the vessel on which Jim sailed was off New York, and they met a brig carrying English prisoners to Halifax to exchange, and received the news from them; a day or two after, they saw the prize towed into New York harbor, "And," says Jim, "you could run a barrow through the sides any where." "Soon after, we met a vessel with the news that Gen. Brock was killed, and I tossed up my hat, and yelled, 'Hurrah for the Yankee cow-boys!'"

Preparations were made on board the *Shepherdess* to make battle at any time, but the mutinous spirit which for some time had been secretly moving some of the crew, incited Jim to make any efforts he could, to injure the British cause; and he states with a great deal of fun and mischief sparkling from his black eyes, which even now have vim enough to do a good turn to a younger body, how he collected rat-tail files, fully intending to spike the English guns if the time ever came when he should be compelled to fight his own countrymen. His patriotism was intense, and although he had been impressed into British service, still he was staunch and true to the Stars and Stripes.

The vessel made for New York, and anchored just off the Highlands, at the entrance to New York harbor. The sight of his own country so excited Jim that he, in desperation, endeavored to sink the vessel, and for the purpose procured an auger, and having found a secure place, set to work to bore a hole in the bottom, bound to sink the entire crew rather than sail any longer in the hated concern. Fortunately, perhaps, for him, his efforts were discovered in time to prevent the wholesale destruction of the ship's men, and but for the intense excitement of the times, and the immediate necessity for the English vessel to make sail, no doubt Jim would have received such punishment as would have at least prevented the publication of this biography.

With fair winds, they reached the rocks of Scilly, off the south-west coast of England, in thirty days; the Captain of the vessel seeing fit to punish Jim for his murderous intentions with but slight reprimand. Here, at Scilly, they found it necessary to procure a supply of provisions, and on making port, eight men, one of whom was Jim, were sent on shore, with a young boy to mind the boat, to procure what they needed. But we will let Prof. Jim tell his own story. He says:

"I pulled after-oar in the boat, for I was always the best oarsman there. It was about dark when we were ordered ashore, and I asked the coxswain (the boy mentioned before) if we might get some beer; having permission, we went up to a corner tavern and went in through the open door, and got our beer. We were all very lame and stiff, for we were not used to walking, but, thinks I to myself, now's the time; so I gave the wink to the fellows, and we just *went for it*, and hobbled out of the back door as fast as ever we could. At the end of half an hour, we heard a drum beat; then said I to the fellows, 'Look out for yourselves,' and we all dropped into a ditch, and just in time, too, for we were hardly still, before a party of men rode by on horseback, and so close were they to us that the dust from the horses' hoofs was scattered over us.

"When the coast was clear, and no one seemed to be stirring, we started on, lame and tired, and moved forward till late in the night, till we found a bright light ahead of us, and we walked towards it. We found it came from a great stone house, which was surrounded by a high stone-wall, and the only entrance was through an arched gate-way shut up by a high iron gate. I called and shouted at the top of my voice, but only managed to stir up a lot of dogs, who yelped, and howled, and barked, with noise enough to waken the neighborhood.

"A woman appeared and called the dogs away, and asked us what we wanted.

"'Who are you?' said she.

"'Yankee deserters,' said I.

"And so she let us in, and stowed us up in the garret, and there we stayed for three days. On the third day, from the garret window we saw the *Shepherdess* sail away, and then we came down. I had on a long blue coat and a pair of English breeches, and the rest of the men were in their sailor dress.

"We went down to the wharf, and there was a ship with good luck for us, for the lash-whip was flying for hands, and we all went aboard and asked if they wanted any help; they were bound for New York.

"'You are Yankees,' said the Captain.

"'Yes,' said the men.

"'You are those deserters from the *Shepherdess*,' said the Captain again.

"'Yes,' replied the men.

"'All right, then, go below and keep out of sight.'"

But Jim stayed on deck, for he was an American, and could only be taken by force, while the other men were Irish, and called themselves Yankees be cause they rather favored the cause of the Americans in the war which was just breaking out.

"Well," continues Jim, "when we had got out to sea, about evening I saw a sail, and said I to the Captain, 'That's the *Shepherdess*.' 'Then hide, all of you,' said he. The men were below, but I got into a locker. By-and-by the *Shepherdess* came along side, and our Captain received the officers on board. The British Lieutenant sat down on the top of the very locker in which I was hid, but he didn't know it, and I was all safe, and after a time they went away, and I never saw them again."

The danger of the men who had escaped with Jim, and of even Jim himself, was very great until he had safely landed in New York. American seamen were impressed wherever they could be taken on the high seas, and Hildreth, in his History of the United States, says that twenty-five hundred of these same impressed sailors, still claiming to be American citizens, and refusing to fight against their country, were committed to close imprisonment. In case of capture, then, Jim and his followers would have had but a sorry chance; and he thinks himself that he had a very narrow escape, for British imprisonment was so severe that its mere suggestion might frighten even sailors on board a vessel of war.

The vessel Jim was now in was the *Caroline*, and she sailed directly for New York, where Jim left her, and was shipped as powder-monkey on board the sloop of war *Hornet*. Fighting had actually begun to be a very earnest thing in the United States, and Cooper, in his Naval History, gives a list of the war vessels which were equipped and sent out from Boston and New York at this time, and mentions the *Hornet* as one of the fleet.

In writing the history of Prof. Jim's connection with the *Hornet*, we find ourselves all at once thrown into contact with statements which eminent historians have pictured in thrilling detail. Wherever the war of 1812 is spoken of, we invariably find that among naval battles of great interest mentioned, the *Hornet* is made noteworthy. These accounts are taken mainly from official reports of the day, presented to the authorities of government by the commanders of the respective vessels engaged, and as the statements are made by responsible persons, we are inclined to accept them without further inquiry.

On the other hand, the present writer finds an old man, wholly unlettered, and with the propensity of his race to magnify and enlarge upon any topic with which they may imagine themselves familiar, uttering statements which we are obliged to authenticate by credible history to assure ourselves that they are true. It is a point of great interest and satisfaction to find his story verified; we tell it as we glean it piecemeal from him, and add the same history as it is given by standard writers like Cooper and Hildreth.

As stated before, Jim was shipped as powder-monkey on board the *Hornet*, but the Captain (Lawrence) soon found out the qualities of his new hand, and that timidity was not his failing, and he soon promoted Jim to a gun on the larboard quarter, where he had an opportunity of seeing and hearing what he would otherwise have missed. He says: "We sailed to the West Indies, and off South America we had an engagement with the *Peacock*, a British vessel of war. We sunk her in twenty-five minutes.

"When the *Peacock* was discovered, another fellow and I were boxing up in the shrouds, and he called out that there was a ship coming along; and there she was, sure enough, and a noble looking thing she was, sir.

"Well, pretty soon the balls began to fly, and I tell you it was hot work; talk about your playing ball, them were the balls as you couldn't put out your hand to catch.

"Well, we sunk her, and lost five of our men inside her, whom the Captain had sent on board to save some of the wounded; but rum and tobacco got the best of them, and as she went down all of a sudden, that was the last of them.

"She came right off us *so*," says old Jim, holding his hands parallel, but the right, representing the *Peacock*, about a foot in the rear of his left hand, "and we came so near together that for a minute the yards locked, and there was an awful crash, and the waves were running high. I stood on the larboard side, with what they called a 'tub' of pistols and hand spikes, and at the first crash a hand spike caught in my wrist, and that is the scar, sir," showing a veritable scar upon his hand. "As the *Peacock* passed, some man in our shrouds up aloft shot her Captain, and he fell on the deck.

"The sterns of the two vessels were near together, and the balls flew like hail, and I got struck by a splinter on the knee, and was sent below, for the blood was streaming down over my foot; but I crawled back on deck again. Our wounded were very few, but a gun '*busted*' and killed some, and some were drowned in the *Peacock*. I remember seeing some men up aloft when she sunk, and they were taken aboard from there."

Cooper's report of this action will throw a little interesting light on Jim's statement. He says: "The *Hornet* sailed from Boston on the 26th of October, 1812, touching at the different rendezvous (so without doubt in the Chesapeake Bay, where Jim went on board) with letters, according to arrangement, arriving off St. Salvador on the 13th of December, and the *Hornet* was sent in to communicate with the consul. She remained off St. Salvador alone for eighteen days, when she was chased into the harbor by the *Montague.* It was late in the evening when the *Montague* approached, and the *Hornet* availed herself of the darkness to wear, and stand out again, passing into the offing without further molestation. Captain Lawrence now hauled by the wind with the intention of going off Pernambuco.

"While the *Hornet* was beating round the Carobana bank, a sail was made on her weather quarter edging down towards her. It was now half-past three P. M., and the *Hornet* continuing to turn to windward with her original intention, by twenty minutes past four the second stranger was made out to be a large man-of-war brig, and soon after she showed English colors.

"As soon as her captain was satisfied that the vessel approaching was an enemy, the *Hornet* was cleared for action, and her people went to quarters. The ship was kept close by the wind, in order to gain the weather gage, the enemy still running free. At 5.10, feeling that he could weather the Englishman, Captain Lawrence showed his colors, and tacked. The two vessels were now standing towards each other, with their heads different ways, both close by the wind. They passed *within half pistol-shot* at 5.25, delivering their broadsides as the guns bore, each vessel using the larboard battery.

"As soon as they were clear, the Englishman put his helm hard up, with the intention to wear short round and get a raking fire at the *Hornet;* but the manœuvre was closely watched, and promptly imitated, and firing his starboard guns, he was obliged to right his helm as the *Hornet* was coming down on his quarter in a perfect blaze of fire.

"The latter closed, and maintaining the admirable position she had got, poured in her shot with such vigor, that a little before 5.40 the enemy not only lowered his ensign, but he hoisted it union down, in the fore-rigging, as a signal of distress. His main-mast soon after fell.

"Mr. Shubrick was sent on board to take possession. This officer soon returned with the information that the prize was the enemy's sloop-of-war *Peacock*, Captain Peake, and that she was fast sinking, having already six feet of water in her hold. Mr. Cormer and Mr. Cooper were immediately despatched with boats to get out the wounded, and to endeavor to save the vessel. It was too late for the latter, though every exertion was made.

"Both vessels were immediately anchored, guns were thrown overboard, shot-holes plugged, and recourse was had to the pumps, and even to bailing, but the short twilight of that low latitude soon left the prize-crew, before the prisoners could be removed. In the hurry and confusion of such a scene, and while the boats of the *Hornet* were absent, four of the Englishmen lowered the stern boat of the *Peacock*, which had been thought too much injured to be used, jumped into it and pulled for land at the imminent risk of their lives.

"Mr. Conner became sensible that the brig was in momentary danger of sinking, and he endeavored to muster the people remaining on board in the *Peacock's* launch, which still stood on deck, the fall of the main-mast and the want of time having prevented an attempt to get it into the water. Unfortunately, a good many of the *Peacock's* people were below, rummaging the vessel, and when the brig gave her last wallow it was too late to save them.

"The *Peacock* settled very easily but suddenly in five and a half fathoms water, and the two American officers, with most of the men and several prisoners, saved themselves in the launch, though not without great exertions. Three of the *Hornet's* people (Jim says *five*) went down in the brig, and nine of the *Peacock's* were also drowned. *Four more of the latter saved themselves by running up the rigging into the foretop*, which remained out of the water after the hull had got to the bottom.

"In this short encounter, the *Peacock* had her

captain and four men killed, and thirty-three wounded. The *Hornet* had one man killed, and two wounded, *in addition to two men badly burned by the explosion of the cartridge.*

"The *Hornet* in the action mustered 135 men fit for duty, the *Peacock* 130."

We quote thus at length, for as the whole battle must have been witnessed by Prof. Jim, he himself indeed, taking an active part in it, every item is of interest to any one who is interested in the life of the venerable janitor.

Cooper further adds, that Captain Lawrence, being overburdened with prisoners and being short of supplies, sailed for New York, and this accords with Jim's statement, that he went directly to New York, where he left the *Hornet* and went on board another vessel.

After leaving the *Hornet* at New York, Jim, not yet wearied with sailor's life and hardships, went on board the first vessel which offered itself. This proved to be a pirate, although Jim asserts that he had no suspicions of its true character till they were fairly out at sea. She was called the "*True blooded Yankee*," and she sailed directly for St. Salvador, Brazil, and Buenos Ayres, where she began a series of robberies on any craft which chanced to fall in her way; but no murders were committed, as the captain only professed to rob, not to murder.

Leaving South America, they went over to the

coast of Spain, and plundered a number of vessels, and in a measure felt that the trip had been very successful, although at one time they narrowly escaped being run down by a Spanish seventy-four, which gave them chase for two days and two nights. They returned to New York, and having rid them selves of their spoils, sailed again for the South American coast. When just outside Sandy Hook, a United States war vessel gave them chase, and pursued them some days, but did not overtake them. The captain of the pirate knew the pursuing vessel as the *Wasp*, one of the fleet which was fitted out for the war at the time the *Hornet* was sent out to the Southern coast.

As they neared the West Indies, they boarded and plundered a ship outward bound from Havana, and the following day captured two more. They pursued a third when near St. Salvador, when a gun-ship gave chase and drove them two days full sail out to sea again.

Instead of returning to their first destined port they sailed for Buenos Ayres, and had a narrow escape from a ship which they mistook in the fog and mist for a trader, but which they suddenly discovered to be a large man-of-war, and they had to "run for it," in sailor language.

Prof. Jim was on this pirate ship for seven months, and at the end of that time made his escape at St.

Salvador, according to his own statement, somewhat in this manner.

Tired and sick of continual plunder, and wearied of the routine of privateer service, he made up his mind, by this time somewhat disciplined by experience, that he would escape at the first port where an opportunity should present itself. It chanced to be at St. Salvador, Brazil. He did not run away the first time he was sent on shore, nor the second, but when his movements were least likely to be suspected he took to his heels, leaving his chest, clothes, money, and all that was due to him from his captain on board the vessel.

He found at last that he could make nobody understand a word he spoke, and he began to be frightened lest he should find that he had chosen the wrong time for making his escape from the privateer. He walked along the street, gazing into store windows or booths as he passed, looking for some face that would give an intelligent smile in return, and would have given up in despair and have considered his case as hopeless, had he not at a fortunate moment met a lady who could talk English, and to whom he imparted his distress. She took pity on him, and having provided food for his comfort, gave him an old suit of clothes, put him on a *poste diligence*, bound along the coast with mail for Buenos Ayres.

If the reader will trace out the line on a map of Brazil he will find, as we did, that Jim's statements are worthy of credence, for he mentions as towns through which he passed on this long and tedious overland journey, *Rio Janeiro* and *Monte Video*. At the latter place he says, "we had to take a boat and cross some sea, or river, and then we were at Buenos Ayres." The "sea or river" was of course the Rio de la Plata, and the only mail line that we can suppose to exist between *St. Salvador* and *Buenos Ayres* must have passed through the large cities mentioned as lying on his route.

From Buenos Ayres he shipped in an American vessel and returned again to New York.

Still of a roving disposition, Jim shipped again, and this time on an American trader, Captain Lorie, bound for China.

They went to Havre de Grace, and sold out their cargo for the purpose of having ready money for trade in teas and silks, but strange to say an old acquaintance of Jim's crosses his path, when his newly adopted vessel had hardly made way for its eastern destination. It was four days from Havre, and a sail made its appearance, which the captain recognized at once, and that it boded him no good; and it seems that the recognition extended to the runaway sailor Jim, for it was the same pirate craft from which he had escaped, the "True blooded Yankee." However, the usually successful privateer this time missed her prey, and the China trip was made in safety.

The land of the Mandarin did not please Jim, and although his opportunities for observation were small, and his present recollection not at all vivid, yet he states very clearly what he remembers.

He says they made port at Canton, but were not allowed to enter the city at all, but all trading was done outside a high protecting wall, around the top of which odd sort of vehicles were driving, and odder looking people walked. The sailors used to venture as far as they dared inside the gates, but were always driven back with great hullaballoos that would have terrified any one, and no one could talk with the Chinamen, for they didn't understand the sailors nor the sailors them.

The lading was tea and silk. After remaining in that port for a month or more, the vessel sailed for New York, making the passage in somewhat over 130 days. Storms and trouble they encountered without end, but after nearly five months voyage they landed their cargo safely in New York city.

After returning from his trip to the East Indies, Jim shipped on board the *Harrison*, bound for France. During the voyage they encountered a terrific storm, which swept over them for three whole days, leaving the decks clear and the vessel scudding under bare poles. Here Jim puts in a little anecdote, which he relates with infinite gusto as illustrating his own bold and impudent manner when in great danger or distress. The captain had given up the vessel as lost, and as a last extremity had called the crew together for general counsel. Pale and terrified faces surrounded the anxious captain as he looked wistfully about this crowd of men, who had placed so much confidence in him as to trust to his guidance over the wide seas; after a few words, explaining the great danger they were in, he asked if any one had any plans to suggest other than had already been tried, or if any one could suggest any means of saving life, if any could possibly be saved in such a raging sea. It seems that before leaving port the vessel had been furnished with a new deck, and the thought popped into Jim's head that this had not perhaps occurred to the captain, and in spite of fear and distress, creaking timbers and raging waves, he shouted at the top of his lungs, "Stick to the new deck, captain." The storm abated, and the crew found no necessity for sticking to the new deck, except as it formed a part of the ship to which it belonged; but the captain lost no opportunity to reprimand Jim for his unbecoming levity, exhibited as it had been at a time when they could scarcely call their lives their own.

III.

"A change came o'er the spirit of my dream."—BYRON.

"A College joke to cure the dumps."—SWIFT.

* * *

Several times Jim made this trip to the French coast, and he became quite familiar with the French people and their customs. He relates how once at Bordeaux he ventured to walk out in the street with one of the waitresses of his boarding house, when they met the girl's lover, a "johnny arms," as he calls him, (probably a *gendarme*,) and the irate lover gave full chase to the offending sailor, "And," says Jim, "I flew for ship board, and the way I ran was just nobody's business, whew! whew!"

Professor Jim never learned the French language, nor even the Spanish, although he had so many opportunities, but then he never could get hold of the right moment for such things, and very calmly replies, if expostulated with, "Why, it aint no kind o' use any how."

Foreigners of all classes he affects to despise, and prizes the true blooded Yankee above all things, except when it proves to be a pirate vessel, and that, one from which he has had to run for his life.

After this memorable voyage Jim began to tire of the high seas, and settled down more to home life, and for a short time acted as sailor, first in a packet plying between Norwich, Conn., and New York, and next as fireman in the steamer *Eagle*, plying between Norwich and New London, and then his sailor life came to an end. Jim left the water to become a landsman, and found work in the stone quarries at Portland, Conn., where he remained for two years, and then for two years more he lived with a gentleman in Middletown as general servant, gardener, and hostler. At the expiration of his service in Middletown he came to Hartford to live, as waiter in the old City Hotel, (kept by a Mr. Bennett,) and while there his active movements and his willingness to do a favor and to show himself ready at any time, won the good will of Mrs. Brownell, who, with the Bishop, was then boarding at the hotel, and he finally became a servant in the Bishop's house, where he remained for a number of years.

Bishop Brownell moved his family from New York to Hartford in 1821, and Prof. Jim asserts that he became a part of the Bishop's household almost at the same time.

The College was founded in 1823, and the care of the morning-bell fell to Jim, and it was some years before the exclusive care of "dust and ashes" fell to his portion.

Pretty well advanced in life, it occurred to the janitor, now settled at steady employment, that the delights of the home circle might as well be his own as well as the comfort of other men about him.

About the same time that Jim came to Hartford to live, a family living on Trumbull street had a slave girl in their employ, who used occasionally to visit some of the friends of the janitor, and there Prof. Jim made her acquaintance. The courtship was not of long duration, and the course of true love ran smoothly, and says Jim, "She had no friends in the world, nor had I, and so we were married," and the couple began housekeeping in a little house on the lot adjoining the college grounds, where the city park now lies.

Jim's attachment to the founder of Trinity College, and to his family was very strong, and he speaks very feelingly of his relations with them all. How he "toted" the children around: how he "'tended to all the marketin', and would let the Bishop do nothing at all. Why, sir, he didn't know nothin' 'bout sugar and groceries, or meat, or vegetables, or nothin', but I'd 'tend the whole of it myself."

At first the college consisted of but one building, *i. e.*, Jarvis Hall, then soon afterwards Seabury Hall was built, and these two buildings formed the entire college for a number of years.

During the time that Bishop Brownell was the presiding officer, Prof. Jim was constantly at the college, excepting one winter, when he went back to the City Hotel, but with the coming spring he returned again to his duties as janitor.

Prof. Jim's college life thus began with the birth of Trinity College, and it is now half a century since that important moment. The most difficult part of his biography to relate lies within these fifty years. The life of a college janitor is, at the best, only routine, and although during so long a time many changes have taken place in the outside world, they do not lie within the sphere which we are describing. The college bell has been the almost constant charge of Jim since his connection with the college, and the responsibility has been faithfully met, as our own experience assures us, and even when "the tongue was not thar," yet Prof. Jim has been on time, and mounting to the belfry would hammer out the call to students, laughing with the best of them. His laughs, however, meant that he was yet even with them.

During the earlier days of his career he was facetiously dubbed Professor, though when and by whom he does not recollect, and the title adheres as firmly as if he had in reality taken his diploma. He says that it is "Dust and ashes" he professes! or in plainer English, that the department of dust and ashes is his peculiar right. Since however he has been unable through the infirmity of years to superintend the "ashes," he has preferred to be called the Professor of secrets, the whole force of this title lying in one of his own sayings, viz: "What you knows, I knows, and nobody else knows." Professing that although he is fully aware of the mischief inherent in college students, yet he has never been guilty of informing the authorities when occasion has presented itself.

His faithful attendance to the bell has been the cause of several poetic effusions from rhyming students, to whom the bell has been a provoking reminder of the call of duty, and it was formerly the delight of the Senior to shout from a window on the morning after class day, while the bell was calling the under class-men to their recitations, "Where's the fire? where's the fire?" One of these poetic seniors contributed the following lines to an early number of the *Tablet*, and we insert them in full.

AFTER CLASS DAY.

Strain well your time-worn hempen rope,
"Professor Jim," both bold and true,
And give your muscles ample scope;
Who cares for college bell or you?

There was a time I heard its peal
With quickened pulse and ravished ear,
But now—ring on, for now I feel,
That you may ring while I lie here

And snore away without remorse,
Or fear of Faculty or Law;
For I have done my College course—
Am independent as a saw.

See how the trembling fellows run,
Juniors, Sophs., and Freshmen too—

While I lie here and see the fun,
And care not, "Jim," for bell or you.

So pull away, my hearty man,
And make her peal out wild and free!
Pull, pull away, pull all you can—
For all your pulling—wakes not me.

Next to the care of the bell it is Prof. Jim's duty to summon students when their presence is required by the Faculty.

Accustomed to dodges of all kinds, nothing will discourage him, and he has been known to take a seat outside the door of a student's room and to sit there for hours, "bound to catch that fellow," if he had to sit there a week, and he is usually successful, for many years' experience has taught him how to proceed with a sure chance of success.

Jim facetiously says that he is on the "war path" when he is hunting for students who are to appear before the Faculty to answer for some misbehavior.

He divided his time between the house duties at the Bishop's and bell-ringing early in the morning at the college, for a number of years, and assisted the established janitor in the "ashes department," till finally he was himself advanced to the important post of head janitor, which position he held faithfully for a period of thirty years; in later days he began to feel the infirmities of old age creeping upon him, and his labors have been materially lightened, and he at the present time rings the bells for recitation and for rising, as he did half a century ago, and besides, lights the fires in the lecture rooms and "blows" the chapel organ.

Many witticisms, sharp and original, have dropped from the mouth of the aged janitor, and if it were possible to collect a memorabilia of these *bons mots* they would be as amusing as Joe Miller's jests, but they are like flashes of light, sparkling for a moment and then lost forever, except when they recur to the memory of some graduate, or to the amused student as he recalls the occasion of the utterance.

Since its foundation there have been eight Presidents of the college, viz: Bishop Brownell, until 1831; Rev. N. S. Wheaton, D. D., from 1831 to 1837; Rev. Silas Totten, D. D., from 1837 to 1848; Rev. John Williams, D. D., an Alumnus of the college, from 1848 to 1853; Rev. D. R. Goodwin, D. D., from 1853 to 1860; Samuel Eliot, LL. D., from 1860 to 1864; Rev. J. B. Kerfoot, D. D., from 1864 to 1866; and since 1866, Rev. A. Jackson, an Alumnus of the college.

Of each and all of these gentlemen Prof. Jim has a vivid remembrance.

From 1851 to 1854 the theological school, subsequently removed to Middletown, was a part of the college, and the theologians used to delight in the discussions which Prof. Jim was always ready to enter into. I am indebted to one of these same theologians, now an eminent clergyman, for the following anecdote:

Prof. Jim was advancing the strongest arguments against the use of ardent spirits, waxing eloquent over the assumed virtue of the patriarchs in this respect, when he was posed for a moment by a student, who asked him "how it was in the case of Noah?"

Jim's reply was soon ready, however.

"Oh!" says he, "there are a good many kinds of *intopsication*, and Noah's was intopsication of spirit."

Another time, while the Professor was in one of the upper windows of a college building, a freshman thought it would be an excellent joke to hide Jim's wheelbarrow, and, unconscious that Jim was watching him all the time, carried it with great effort up stairs, and piled wood from the wood-pile over it. When he had finished, Jim's head came forward, and in tones of withering sarcasm he said: "*O, you fresh!!*" The mortified freshman actually carried the wheelbarrow back to the place from which he had brought it, and we would be willing to wager troubled Professor Jim no more that year.

One of the earlier Presidents greatly enraged the janitor by interfering, as he termed it, with his (the janitor's) rights. Anger rankled in the offended servitor's bosom, but he had no means of appeasing the pain till on one occasion he shot the bolt directly home in this way. The newly elected President accosted him one morning with, "Good day, James; well, you have lived to see quite a number of changes in the college since you've been here, — Presidents in all, haven't you?" "Yes," said Jim, "Yes, sir, I've lived to see — Presidents over this 'ere college, and," drawing his form as erect as possible, "*I hope to live to see another.*" He had had his revenge (!), and it was very sweet to him, and he glories over it to this day.

From the earliest records Prof. Jim has been a prominent personage at Class-Day celebrations, and it is an established custom to give the worthy janitor some substantial memento before the class breaks up, and the responses of Jim are among the pleasantest reminiscences of that crowning day of the college course. Once he used to fill the pipes and distribute the punch to the class while the literary exercises were proceeding, but of late years he has been obliged to yield these *last* duties to younger and sprightlier assistants, and he retains his seat in the circle with the class.

The presiding officer of the day tenderly escorts the old grey-headed man to his post of honor, and again escorts him to the scene of the ivy-planting, every one present yielding a respectful deference to the years and the associations connected with this faithful servitor.

A representative of the class, before the close of

the exercises, speaks the word of parting, and tenders a purse to Prof. Jim, and he, half in humor half in sorrow, gives vent to words which must be heard to be well appreciated. The mingled pathos and wit with which the old janitor endeavors to express his gratitude, his sorrow at parting with friendly faces, and to give his advice which experience has taught him all young men need ere they undertake their journey by themselves, altogether, render the production one of interest.

In the absence of all available data we are obliged to content ourselves with those reports we have by us, but scanty as they prove to be they are sufficient to show the tenor of Prof. Jim's remarks.

We are pleased to be able to give in full two of the speeches in which he responds to the well-wishers of the graduating class. The earliest account we can find of a class-day entertainment is of the summer of 1855, when a purse filled with *gold* was presented to the venerable Professor by the class graduating that year. The presentation and address was made through Mr. Geo. A. Woodward, and Prof. Jim is reported as replying "with much earnestness and ability."

In the summer of 1863, a correspondent of the *Hartford Evening Press* reported in full the response of Jim after the presentation of the customary purse; (it was not of gold this time.)

J. S. Smith of Randolph, Vt., made the presentation and Prof. Jim replied:

"While I've got to be deprived o' these young gentlemen, very near and dear friends, you, young ladies, has got to lose your armor bearers! You have treated 'em so handsomely an' smiled upon 'em so sweetly, that you've kept them when they had ort to be a studyin'.

"I done all I could to have 'em study when they ort to, but they cooden resis' your smiles. But I won't put no more on you than you can bear.

"Gentlemen, you has been very kind to me, an' our communion has been sweet together, our words has been soft, an' what you know I knows, an' nobody else knows.

"But we've got to take our *departur!* What will become of you? the Lord knows. Some may go to the sandy shores of Arabia, some on you to the tropical wilds of Africa—its your own fault if you ain't fitted to travel to *any part o' the state!* The Lord bless you—you knows I always felt a warm interest in your soul's welfare an' worked for your salvation.

"You call me professor, an' so you may. I'm professor o' secrets. What you tell me I don't tell. How you worked and studied all night arter you'd been off, and worried for fear you wooden get your conditions.

"How you had to be dragged out by the heels from under the bed, sometimes to go and visit the faculty.

"How you got along nicely till you run against *chronics*. Chronics was hard.

"But Chronics is gone and Eucly is gone. It's your your own fault if your mind ain't furnished with a good edication to go anywhere.

"I thank you for this purse. No matter how little it is, no matter how great it is, it aint so precious as friends. A man that hain't got a cent in his pocket and has a near and dear friend, is rich—he's got somebody that cares for him. If it's gold it will canker; if it's silver it will rust; if it's copperheads —you know what becomes o' them. But friendship lasts allers, I trus you'll allers be benevolent—your hand open always to resist the needy.

"Our communion has been sweet, but we've got to take our departur.

"Where ere you go may the Lord bless yer—may these sweet ladies keep the pairs o' gloves you give 'em till you come back. You know I always had an interest in your salvation—the Lord bless yer."

A correspondent to a Philadelphia paper, in the summer of 1865, relating the events of class day at Trinity, notes Prof. Jim in such pleasant words that we quote them in full, feeling assured that they will recall to every graduate of the college our hero *in propria persona*.

"The Professor is one of the institutions of

the College, and if you are not already acquainted with him you ought to be and I will endeavor to make you. He has been called janitor, bell ringer, &c., for almost forty years; is a fine looking specimen of an ancient African, black as jet, grey-headed, good-looking and intelligent. He wore on this solemn occasion a dress coat and silk hat, and carried in his hand an enormous gold-headed cane, the gift of a former class. His oration was at this, as at all times, the most remarkable, if not the most classic feature of the whole entertainment.

"The mixture of Ethiopian wit, piety, and eloquence was so droll that it was momentarily greeted with perfect roars of laughter. When he meant to be most solemn, he excited most merriment. But the old Professor, in no wise abashed, kept steadily on, exhorting and thanking and counselling his "young frens," giving expression to whatever came uppermost in his mind, without the least regard to grammar, arrangement, or punctuation until he had had his say.

"Among other things quite as good, but they have escaped my memory, he referred very tenderly to the 'canopy of time,' 'the shores of this College,' and 'this here beautiful canvass' (campus).

"He declared, in a very impressive manner, that this would be his last appearance 'upon that place,' but as he has made the same declaration, just so solemnly too, every class day for the last twenty years, the sentiment failed to excite the tears of his auditory.

However the end must come to the venerable James. When it does come may he be kindly dealt with and made happy forever."

From another correspondent we quote the speech of the occasion in full.

SPEECH.

" Gentlemen of de class of '65 : I'se very happy at dis time to meet you. Let me say at dis time that I have to regret the *loss*. I desire to know, 'fore I go any further, if the editor of the *Times* is here [he stood within a few feet of him], I want to say, if he is, that even a poor ignorant man like me might have told him something better to write than he did las' clas' day. (Laughter.)

" Gentlemen of '65 : Your secrets is mine. What you knows I know. Though you stopped up the key-holes with putty, an' froze up de bell, no matter. *I* was bound you should'nt lose a recitation, if I had to take the door off de hinges. I allers get through somehow.

" Gentlemen : We never had no difficulty. All you treated me as gentlemen. Ladies, *you* will remember the class of '65—you'se got a good many friends among 'em.

" There sits a young man whose father entered college and graduated *with honor and dignity to his parents*, and allers instructed him in his duty.

"Gentlemen: What is that, and that? (pointing to the vacant chairs of Haynes and Lewis, draped in black). There's something gone. Precious souls! precious souls! Remember, gentlemen, you are now in de flower of your youth. You're soon goin' to leave this college, this splended *canvas*—don't neglect to make acquaintance with the Supreme Being.

"Oh, my beloved friends, who has been instructed in de class, *in* de canopy of Heaven, or on de *shores* of Trinity College! (Sensation.)

"Gentlemen: I hold in my hand (lifting his gold-headed cane) something presented to me in 1864, that I prize above all my heart. I stand before you in my ignerance—'scuse me.

"O my beloved class, *whar are you goin'?* (Laughter and applause.) You may enter de ministry, you may enter de lor—wherever you go, remember de instructions you received here. O these glorious walls—the chimes o' dem bells. It's a wonder dey don't ring out peace to your beloved souls.

"Gentlemen: I've had to dig de putty out de keyholes with my jack-knife. But, Prof. Jim, as you call him, would go through de walls but I'd have you out. It was a glory to me when you work all night to freeze up de bell, thinking to lay in your beds in de morning, but I'd bring you out.

"Ladies and Gentlemen: I never had no difficulty with a student. We allers run together. What they knew I knew, and what they didn't know I could tell 'em! This is the last Class Day I expect to be here.

"Gentlemen, you are celebrating your last Class Day. Whar are your faders and moders? Ar' dey here to enjoy dis occasion so happy wid you?—to go out wid you into a world of temptations and sin, and guide you along? If not, I warn you of de temptatations dat beset young men of your character.

"The high privileges that has been granted to you and de benefit of a Supreme Being you ought to appreciate as gentlemen! Gentlemen, I bid you all a final farewell; I could say much more, but time won't admit."

The presentation of the purse this year was made by G. A. Coggeshall, of South Portsmouth, R. I.

The class of '69 presented him with a silver watch in place of the customary purse. Jim's reply is not reported, but it was said to be full of sly hits and one of his very happiest. Mr. W. B. Buckingham, of South Carolina, represented his class in this presentation.

So Class Day is a bright period in Prof. Jim's life; and yet, as he truly says, there is every probability that he will see but few more of these pleasant celebrations, and Class Day will hardly seem a Class Day without him. It is a wonderful thing to see a living servant who for fifty long years has faithfully fulfilled his duties in one house or one family; and it is not to be wondered at that the Alumni of Trinity feel proud of Prof. Jim, and that strangers learning his history look upon him with profound interest. Such a personage as he, will rarely be met with wherever we may go, and every class for which this aged janitor has shown his respect and to whom he has given his parting blessing will hold it among their fondest recollections that "*Prof. Jim*" was a participator in *their* Class Day.

One memorable event in the life of the janitor remains to be recorded.

In the campaign of 1867 he was duly nominated Vice President of the United States, somewhat in this wise. It was upon the occasion of a visit to the college, of Daniel Pratt, the Great American Traveler. A local paper describes the affair thus:

" Daniel Pratt, the celebrated traveler, has again honored our city with his presence. Yesterday afternoon, he spoke before a delighted audience at Trinity College. The oration was a highly polished, scholarly affair, abounding in flowers of rhetoric and striking similes. At the conclusion of his oration, he was unanimously nominated for the Presidency in 1868. Mr. Pratt modestly accepted the honor and proceeded to define his position, and establish his platform.

" HON. JAMES WILLIAMS, commonly called 'Prof. Jim,' was nominated for Vice President. Mr. Pratt was very uneasy about the nomination as he feared Mr. Williams was not legally qualified, as to age, etc.

but on being assured that he was of a suitable age, and that he had been a resident graduate of the College for the last twenty-one years, he consented to Mr. Williams' nomination. He further said that in case anything should transpire still he could exercise his veto power.

"It is proprosed by some of our leading citizens to engage Mr. Pratt, regardless of expense, to deliver a course of lectures on American History, the potato rot, etc. By his varied attainments acquired by extensive travels, Mr. Pratt is among the first orators of the country."

We did not hear that Prof. Jim was elected.

As we close these few chapters let us review for a moment the biography we have thus scantily passed over. James Williams first appears as a slave boy in the vicinity of New York City eighty-three years ago, next a hostler, then a fugitive from his home and a sailor in a trading vessel. Time passes on and he is impressed into the British service, then runs away in a romantic manner and is afterwards shipped on board a well-known naval vessel which figures extensively in the war of 1812. After this he visits in his travels, Spain, France, makes a long trip to the East Indies, to China, and then returns to New York. Before this he had been along the shores of Africa, both on the South Atlantic and in the Mediterranean, then to Turkey and to Greece. He visits South America as a sailor on board a pirate vessel and makes a romantic escape at San Salvador. He travels about from place to place and sees and hears the most wonderful things, till at length we find him settled as janitor at Trinity College, and growing old with that institution, becoming himself an interesting personage in its history. He saw the walls of the College rise and, strange to say, lives to see them taken down again. He has witnessed the planting of many ivies which have grown from the simple slip to the wide spreading vines, and he lives to see them cut down at the roots and taken away. He has witnessed the graduation of six hundred and fifty students from his adopted home, and he outlives one hundred and thirty of that number. What an experience his has been!

For a number of years he has been an active member of the Methodist Society to which he joined himself. In fact he was one of the original founders of the African Zion Methodist Church in this city nearly fifty years ago, and he feels that it is part and parcel of himself; he is as revered and his counsels taken as much to heart as if he were the regular preacher to the congregation; and indeed the venerable janitor is duly respected by every one with whom he is acquainted. He is polite, and has a pleasant word to say at all times.

Long may his memory live with those to whom his name and face are most familiar. Wherever the graduate of Trinity goes, wherever the memory of Trinity College remains green, there we feel assured will linger a recollection of the Prince of College Janitors,

PROFESSOR JIM.

ADDENDA.

After the manuscript of this work was ready for the press a letter was received per the Editor of the Hartford *Courant* from the Great Grandson of Col. Robert, Jim's master. The letter is by permission given here. It confirms Prof. Jim's statement fully and adds one more witness to the reliability of the aged janitor's memory. The letter is addressed to the *Courant*, advance sheets of the biography appearing in that paper in March.

NEW YORK, March 29th, 1873.

Editor Hartford Courant:

DEAR SIR.

I have just read with much interest in the *N. Y. Evening Post*, copied from your journal, an account of the whereabouts of Aaron Burr after the duel with General Hamilton. I take pleasure in verifying Professor Jim's statements as far as my memory serves me, from the frequent accounts given me by my father, the late Philip Rhinelander Robert, Pomora Hall, Yonkers, N. Y. I do not recollect James Williams as he probably moved East before my time. I however recollect *Hannibal* very well, who was probably in the service of my Grandfather, Col. John Robert, at the time Professor Jim was.

* * * * * * *

JOHN F. ROBERT.

6*

After receiving this letter an immediate inquiry was made after "*Hannibal*," and on questioning Prof. Jim it was found the individual in question was a brother-in-law to the janitor, and that he lived but a short distance from his house. An intelligent man was found, polite and ready to answer as far as lay in his power any questions that might be put to him.

He had been a slave, the property of Mr. Blackwell, the son of the gentleman who owned the property known as Blackwell's Island. Mr. Blackwell's estate was next adjoining that of Col. Robert, and it was about two years after the death of the Colonel that he became acquainted with Prof. Jim's sister whom he afterwards married.

It was the second year after the estate had been settled, and Jim and his sister had left Yonkers, that they received news that Jim had run away. It was supposed at first that he had gone to Nyack to visit his father, but as he was not found there, opinions were divided between the "East" and "the sea." At any rate his friends neither heard from him or saw him again till the year after the emancipation of slaves in New York state, which was in 1817.

Professor Jim's father was a slave belonging to Mr. Pugh, of Nyack, but he was allowed his freedom when he was come of age, and for years worked as stone cutter in quarries near his former master's home. His children were allowed to visit him occasionally and he saw them several times a week till the family was finally broken up at the death of Col. Robert, and the children were scattered. We are able to get at Professor Jim's age more accurately by relying upon the statement of Hannibal. His problem is worked out mathematically thus.

Hannibal's wife was one year older than her husband, and he is seventy-three years old. He married the fifth child, and Jim was the third, and there was a difference of two years between the ages of the children. Prof. Jim is therefore eighty years old.

A second letter from Mr. Robert still further verifies Prof. Jim's statements and adds a few interesting facts to those already given.

" The Robert estate at the time Jim was a part of the Colonel's family consisted of 500 acres; the old family manor " Pomora Hall " is now in the possession of Sidney B. Morse, Esq., (son of the late Prof. Morse).

Mr. Robert very kindly sent to the writer two autograph letters written by Aaron Burr to the late Colonel Robert. Their contents show plainly the relations existing between the two gentlemen. We have permission to publish them and are glad to be able to, for they have never been placed in any previous collection of Burr's letters.

The first letter is dated New York, May, 1800, and is not as clear to understand as the second.

DEAR SIR:

The letter from Mr. Prevost and the paper inclosed by him will show you the intentions of your adversaries. As there is no prospect that the trial would come on, there would be no other use in my attendance than the pleasure of passing a day with you in the country. Unfortunately I have no time for amusement. I regret your disappointment and my own, and am always affec'y

Your friend,

A. BURR.

The second bears the date, New York, July 28th, 1802.

DEAR SIR:

My pasture is completely eaten up and there being none on the Island that is good, I send Harry with two horses to your care. Let them run in some good pasture where there are some bushes to brush off the flies—These singular look animals were made a present to me in S. Carolina. They are full-blooded Arabians, and were brought from the western side of the Mississippi. From their appearance you would not suppose that they cost 800 Dolls.

Yet such I am told is the fact. You may use them in your phæton if you please, but pray take care that they are not rode by negroes.

Your affec. friend and servant,

A. BURR.

COL. JOHN ROBERT.

Professor Jim remembers the ponies well and describes them as spotted red and white.

"Harry," mentioned in the letter was his mother's brother.

"Now how strange," says Jim, "ain't it that them ar' letters should be kept till this time, and about them ponies ?"

From among numerous letters received while writing this biography, the following is selected, for it shows how in his station Jim's influence was exerted in behalf of the College.

St. George's—

SCHENECTADY, April 2d, 1873.

Dear Sir :

The lives of eminent men are often barren of action and incident. If such proves to be the case in regard to the distinguished individual, for whose biography you request me to furnish some materials, it will not be thought an argument against his greatness.

It is a very humble memorial which I have to send. But as Boswell thought it important to narrate his first meeting with Dr. Johnson, and as Lockhart is particular to describe Sir Walter Scott, as he first saw him; so I may reproduce the occasion of my first sight and knowledge of Professor Jim.

It was some years before I entered Trinity, or thought of doing so, and in my native town, Chatham, now Portland, Conn. Bishop Brownell, who had then moved to Hartford and assumed the presidency of the College, was to make a visitation to our Parish Church. On the Sunday morning when he was expected, I stood, a mere boy, among the people, who, as was then too much the custom in the country, gathered outside the church door, awaiting the arrival of the minister.

This morning the number was, of course, increased by the expectation of seeing the Bishop. In due time he appeared, in the two wheeled carriage—gig, it was called—in which he then, before the day of railroads, made many of his visitations.

He was driven by Jim, sitting by his side. I can see now at the distance of more than forty years the grand style in which Jim cracked his whip over the horse's head, and wheeled the gig as he neared the steps of the door, just avoiding them, having in his professional mind, perhaps Horace's *meta fervidis evitata rotis.* And I shall never forget the self-satisfied air with which he alighted, nor the ease and grace of manner with which he afterwards assisted the Bishop out of the carriage and with a wave of the hand passed him over to the Rector and Church Wardens who were there to receive him.

Bishop Brownell was always a marked man in his personal appearance. But, at that time, he was in the prime of his bodily presence and manly beauty, and the accompaniment of the graceful and deferential servant on that occasion, added much to the dignity and consequence of the Bishop in my youthful eyes. Indeed I do not know but the little incident had its influence in turning my feet to Trinity, when afterwards I determined to go to college. I am sure at least, there was a peculiar aesthetical charm about the Institution, as it began under the accomplished Bishop, who observed himself, and impressed upon others, "the fair humanities of old religion."

Yours, &c.,

WM. PAYNE.

Mr. C. H. Proctor.

In reply to a letter written to Dr. J. Bernard Gilpin, Halifax, Nova Scotia, a graduate of '31, the following communication was received, which must be of exceeding interest to every alumnus of Trinity

College; not so much because Professor Jim was a janitor in the writer's day, in fact he seems hardly to have been known as he was then the Bishop's servant, but because the letter mentions incidents as they then occurred, and persons who since that time have become widely known in cultivated circles as Bishops, Poets, or Authors.

HALIFAX, 29th March, 1873.

DEAR SIR:

More than forty and odd years have passed since I left Hartford. I joined in 1828, freshmen, third term, and graduated 1831.

My first year was famous for the great *barring-out*. Some great depredations having been done in town, the magistrates summoned by subpœna every student and caused them to purge themselves by oath. Taken by surprise they all submitted, except Hugh Peters, son of Judge Peters, who resisted. Coming back to college, the students became indignant, thinking the faculty should have protected them rather than have connived at it, and at eleven o'clock lecture, barred college and chapel, allowing none to enter. The Bishop broke down the south section door with a fence pole from the west lane, and Dr. Doane had a black suit ruined by dirty stuff thrown from the windows. The attack ceased, but when the evening bell rung all went to prayers as usual, and no notice was taken of it. So illegal an act I hope would not be tolerated by the public now.

As regards our habits at that day, I can only say we had three daily lectures ; dined at twelve o'clock and took tea at five. On Saturday morning the lecture was before breakfast, only.

Saturday was usually employed by the students at the various societies, where they discussed all topics but religion. In after life I have often remembered the care, the writers, the compositions, and the order of these meetings; but I was not of them, and being an English boy, and then wearing crape for the King (George IV) I could not stand the washy floods of classic liberty and death to tyrants which flowed out, I cut them and spent my Saturdays in Summer in rambling over the hills with my gun, or walking over Rocky Hill (as I now recollect it, an elevation of Trap through Triasic sand-stone), or bathing in the Connecticut. We usually swam across it.

In Winter we skated on the Hog river. Mile after mile have I glided on its reaches, with the red squirrel following me on the banks. As winter wore on, we took to the Connecticut. Thomas Suckley (yet alive I think) and myself, once left Hartford, on skates, the bells as was the custom ringing high twelve, went to Middletown, and returned. Opposite *Mother Bunce's* at Wethersfield, twilight caught us, and for fear of air holes, we walked into the city. We considered we would have reached home by five, as we timed ourselves at other times to fifteen minutes from Wethersfield home. We thought we made fifty miles in five hours, or nearly.

The Junior exhibition, and parts of Commencement, were studied for with the greatest ardor, and our *orations*, so called then, were spoken in black silk gowns which were hired from Stockbridge the tailor. Notwithstanding undergraduates are not entitled to sleeves, unless King's scholars, they all had the pudding or full Doctor's robe sleeve.

Of the undergraduates of my years who have arrived to fame, Park Benjamin might be seen lifted on his pretty barb mare by his servant for his daily ride.

Bailey, R. C. Bishop of Baltimore, was the handsomest and most gentle nurtured youth in the College. Vail, now I think a Bishop, joined, a weakly boy, studied muscular Christianity and left a strapping fellow. He gained more than a good degree.

The Southern General Hill I think was my classmate. Cornwall walked off with the valedictory from two or three of us who were bracketed number two.

Of the notable outsiders then seen in the streets of Hartford, Imley was the personification of wealth; Wadsworth lived in good form at his mansion in town, but his toy castle already wore the look of a forgotten plaything; Mrs. Sigourney wrote, and tried in vain to colonize her side of our river with squirrels which abounded on ours; Prentice daily sat on the steps of the U. S. Hotel, and "Fanny Fern" and her brother N. P. Willis were frequent visitors to our city.

Dr. Hawes, even then was gray, but erect and firm in his saddle, and might have been seen almost daily putting his sturdy brown cob with a crooked tail through all weathers and roads. Miss Beecher, too, had a good mount and often led a troup of fair Amazons through pretty rough skies. The Governor's Guard with their Major at their head on horseback, in their cocked hats, long tailed coats and black cloth gaiters to the knee, looked as if they might have just returned from Still Water or Saratoga.

I send you also a yellow old paper with dates, which describes the room of a student of that day.

* * * * * * *

I remain yours very truly,

J. BERNARD GILPIN.

Mr. C. H. Proctor.

DIARY.

My own room in College, 1830, *Nov.* 26.

Perhaps one of these days, looking back through a tedious and ill spent life, I may esteem these days happy which I am now in such haste to pass through, and that whenever this takes place, I may have some memorial wherewith to refresh my memory, I now write a faithful and accurate description of my room, No. 31 Washington College, Hartford, Conn., as it is this evening.

It is a room perhaps 20 ft. by 12 ft. The bed stands in a recess on the right side, across which a curtain is drawn excluding it entirely from view; one window looks out upon the west; directly opposite to it is an open stove of the kind called 'Franklin,' with a high and broad pipe reaching within a few inches of the ceiling where it enters into the wall. On this pipe is depicted with chalk, a human skeleton. I roomed alone and strange as it may appear, though repeatedly requested by the Profs. to remove this unseemly sight, I could never do it, it seemed as if I should remove some old companion. The stove is firmly based upon a hearth of brick, around and upon which are lying a pair of tongs, shovel, poker, broom, bellows, hammer, &c., in a state of disorder which to look upon would be death to a notable housewife.

My furniture consists of half a dozen chairs, a bureau, and table; the latter stands before the fire, upon it I am now writing. The books lying at this moment upon it are Endfield's Philosophy, Political Economy, Simson's Euclid, Tylton's History, Blair's Chronology, Ramsay's Universal History, The Bible, (I am reading Ramsay, and these last mentioned books have at different periods been taken down from my book shelf as references when I met with anything I thought misstated or not sufficiently enlarged upon; once taken down it is some time before they find their way back,) an English and

French Dictionary, an atlas, Morse's geography (in criticising a classmate's composition some weeks since I had occasion to use this,) and lastly "Studies of Poetry," containing extracts from Chaucer down ward to Percival, Bryant, and Doane.

I am no great lover of poetry as this sufficiently shows, to take up with extracts instead of the whole, yet thanks to the kind age in which we live, I can now talk as learnedly of the ancient and modern poets as the poor wretch who has delved through the whole of them, for he will only talk of the finest passages and I have got them all in this book.

Now for my ornaments.

My walls are hung with prints, two of Peter Tertu's two hundred years old, full of wild and unearthly figures, with beasts and monsters. Another, artist unknown, allegorical of something connected with the discovery of America, I never could tell exactly what. The heathen divinities are all there, and a great stiff figure clothed in Roman armor, nevertheless with a full-bottom wig on; a head of the surviving Horatio, from David, and a languishing lithographic French beauty; these two hang near each other and admirably set each other off, the one all whiskers, beard and mustache, fierce and bloody looking, the other entirely free from the least expression whatever.

Besides these I have several pictures; a head in oils of an old man with a voluminous beard; a sketch of the ruined tower of Newport, and two fancy sketches valuable on account of the hand that delineated them. These last are not stationary occupiers of the wall; in summer I move my table to the open window, and they follow me to that part of the room; In winter I get before the fire and they come too.

Two busts, Franklin and Washington, look down from their respective pedestals. Several hanging shelves hold my books and they are surmounted by an ear of corn maize. I always liked the looks of an ear of maize, considering it abstractly without thinking of its utility there is something to me beautiful in its form, and so I plucked one from the fields and placed it over my book-case and there it is now with its husk all dry and withered.

A broken looking-glass occupies another portion of the walls and near it is the plume of my late military chum, which occupied a place formerly in his *Phalanx* cap; his pike is resting against the wall hard by. At some distance from it are a pair of skates; my shooting apparatus should be with them but I have lent it. At the opposite side are sundry pairs of shoes and boots; my hat, cap, and several pairs of gloves together with a pile of books, a napkin, a comb and several other articles cover the top of the bureau; an umbrella stands near it. The window seat is spread with some half dozen minerals I have collected in my walks, a hair brush, a hone, a pair of snuffers and two books, and my cloak lies over the back of a chair and a coat upon it. And this is a faithful description of my room, save that I have forgotten to mention in their right places, a boot-jack and a hickory stick. With what different feeling shall I read this twenty years hence.

I forgot to mention the room was neatly papered, and that some former occupant in a bit of patriotism had written "Liberty" in characters broad and long upon the ceiling.

J. B. G.

www.ingramcontent.com/pod-product-compliance
Lightning Source LLC
Chambersburg PA
CBHW030003030726
47499CB00008B/2869
* 9 7 8 3 3 3 7 0 5 4 3 0 4 *